LITTLENOSE THE HERO

Littlenose, the naughty but well-meaning
Neanderthal boy, has suddenly become a
hero! After so many adventures where
things go wrong he has at last achieved
the status he deserves . . . Or does he
deserve it? When he helps his father out
of a deep pit the rest of the tribe praise
his good sense and bravery; but who dug
the pit in the first place?

How Littlenose accidentally became a
hero is just one of his many adventures
featured in this book.

Littlenose was invented for John Grant's own children, but was soon entertaining millions more when he first appeared on Jackanory in 1968.

The Neanderthal boy whose pet was bought in a mammoth sale, whose mother is in despair at the rough treatment he gives his furs, and whose exasperated father sometimes threatens to feed him to a sabre-toothed tiger, is everybody's favourite.

Besides gaining wide acceptance in Great Britain, the Littlenose stories have been translated into German, French, Italian, Dutch, Spanish and Japanese.

More Littlenose titles available from BBC/Knight

Littlenose
Littlenose's Birthday
Littlenose the Marksman
Littlenose the Joker
Littlenose Moves House

LITTLENOSE
THE
HERO

John Grant

Illustrated by the author

BBC/KNIGHT

Copyright © John Grant 1971
First published 1971 by the British Broadcasting Corporation
This edition published 1985 by the British Broadcasting
Corporation/Knight Books
Second impression 1985

British Library C.I.P.

Grant, John *1930*–
   Littlenose the hero.
   I. Title
   823′.914[J]   PZ7

ISBN 0–340–37236–2
     (0–563–20375–7 BBC)

*The characters and situations in this book are entirely imaginary and
bear no relation to any real person or actual happening*

This book is sold subject to the condition that it shall
not, by way of trade or otherwise, be lent, re-sold,
hired out or otherwise circulated without the
publisher's prior consent in any form of binding or
cover other than that in which it is published and
without a similar condition including this condition
being imposed on the subsequent purchaser.

Printed and bound in Great Britain for the British
Broadcasting Corporation, 35 Marylebone High Street,
London W1M 4AA and Hodder and Stoughton
Paperbacks, a division of Hodder and Stoughton Ltd.,
Mill Road, Dunton Green, Sevenoaks, Kent (Editorial
Office: 47 Bedford Square, London WC1B 3DP) by
Richard Clay (The Chaucer Press) Ltd.,
Bungay, Suffolk

Littlenose the Musician

Long, long ago in the Ice Age, tribes of
Neanderthal folk lived in caves and hunted
wild animals for food. Littlenose was a boy
in one of these tribes. A tribe was like a very
large family with all the members related to
each other, so Littlenose had a great many
aunts and uncles. One uncle was Littlenose's
particular favourite. He liked his other
relatives, and loved his father and mother
very much, but not one of them was as
special as Uncle Redhead.

To begin with, he had flaming red hair,
with a beard to match, unlike the other
Neanderthals, who were very dark. Then,
he could do the most remarkable things.
He could light a fire by *rubbing sticks* as well

as by striking flints! He could make painted pictures of animals! *And* he could tell stories.

He would sit for hours and recount strange and sometimes terrifying tales of the barren lands to the north, where the musk oxen roamed, the white bears hunted, and icy rivers flowed from the great Ice Cap. Or perhaps he might describe the sunny land to the south where fish swam in a warm sea, and the fruit was bigger and sweeter than anyone could imagine.

Uncle Redhead was also very generous. He never visited without bringing gifts. It might be new flints for Father, a beautiful fur from some strange animal for Mother, and for Littlenose? Well, he could never guess, but it was always something strange and exciting.

One morning, Father sat mending a spear, while Mother was patching a pair of Littlenose's furs. Father looked very gloomy. Uncle Redhead was back again.

Father looked at Mother. "After all, he's

YOUR brother," he said.

"Step-brother," replied Mother, "and it's not my fault he's so clever."

"That's just the trouble," said Father. "He's too clever by far. It's not right. If you ask me, there's something odd about him . . . a touch of –" (and here Father lowered his voice to a whisper) – "a touch of Straightnose!"

"Straightnose!" gasped Mother.

"All these tricks of his," went on Father. "What other Neanderthal man can swim, for instance? Or make fire with sticks? And his wanderings! He doesn't live in a cave. He doesn't belong to a tribe. He's not respectable."

"But he's so kind," said Mother, "and Littlenose adores him."

"Littlenose also adores his mammoth," snorted Father, "but at least Two-Eyes doesn't put crazy notions into the boy's head."

At that moment Littlenose trotted up with Two-Eyes.

"Where's Uncle Redhead?" he asked.

"He went out hunting early this morning," said Mother. "He's a very good hunter."

"Too good," muttered Father, darkly.

At that moment, there came a loud shout, and Uncle Redhead strode out of the trees, a haunch of venison on his shoulder.

"Hullo, there," he called. "This is all I could carry. I've hung the rest of the meat in a tree where the foxes can't get it. We can collect it later."

"What a good idea," said Mother. Father only grunted.

"Uncle Redhead! Uncle Redhead!" shouted Littlenose. "You haven't given me my present yet!"

"Littlenose!" exclaimed Mother, but Uncle Redhead only laughed.

"You're quite right to remind me, lad, but I hadn't forgotten. We're going to fetch it now."

Taking Littlenose by the hand, Uncle Redhead strode away up the river bank. Littlenose had to run to keep pace with his uncle's long stride, but after a little while they turned away from the river, and Uncle Redhead said, "This'll do, I think."

Littlenose looked around puzzled. "But my present," he wailed.

"All right, all right," said Uncle Redhead. "In a moment. Just sit here and watch carefully."

Littlenose sat down on a boulder.

Uncle Redhead walked over to a clump of tall hemlock, which waved and nodded its creamy flower heads in the breeze. Very carefully, he took his flint knife and cut a handful of the stalks. He sat down beside Littlenose and said: "Now, watch."

He took a jointed stem, and cut it short just above a joint; then he slit the stem part way down its length, and handed it to Littlenose.

"Now," he said, "blow!"

Rather puzzled, Littlenose put the end of the stalk in his mouth and blew hard. He almost dropped it as it gave out a loud droning sound. He blew it again, and again it made the sound. Littlenose was delighted. He blew long notes. He blew short notes. He blew loudly. And he blew very softly.

He stopped for breath, and found that Uncle Redhead had been busy with more stalks. They were each of different thicknesses, and when Littlenose blew them, they all made different notes. He was so excited he couldn't speak. He wanted to go on blowing and blowing. But his uncle took them from him, and carefully bound them side by side with strips of bark. Then Littlenose found he could easily blow them one after the other, or even two together, and make the most wonderful music. He pranced up and down, blowing his pipes with great gusto, so that the birds stopped chirping to listen, and small animals peered from among the leaves and branches at the marvellous sound.

At last, Littlenose dropped breathlessly on to his rock.

"Uncle Redhead," he gasped, "this is the most wonderful present I ever had."

"I'm glad you like it," said his uncle, "but come along; it's time we were getting home."

When they arrived at the cave, they found that quite a crowd had gathered. Everyone looked very worried, even frightened, and

11

they all began shouting to Uncle Redhead
and Littlenose, "Did *you* hear it? What was
it?"

"What was what?" asked Littlenose.

"The noise," they all said. "You must
have heard it! It came from up the river. A
strange whistling and droning, like wind in
the treetops, and bees swarming, and . . ."

"Oh, you mean like this," said Littlenose,
and pulling his pipes from under his furs he
blew merrily up and down the scale.

Everyone shrank back fearfully. "What is
it?" they asked.

"Uncle Redhead made it for me," said
Littlenose. "It makes music." And he blew
it again.

"Uncle Redhead," muttered Father, as
the crowd dispersed. "I might have known!"

At lunch, Uncle Redhead announced that
he was leaving that afternoon.

"Got to keep moving along, you know,"
he said, and while Father looked very

12

relieved, Littlenose almost cried with disappointment.

The weeks after Uncle Redhead's departure went by, and to everyone's relief, Littlenose gradually forgot about his pipes. In any case, Father had said that he was only to play them where no one could hear, which was difficult, as the piercing notes carried for a very long way indeed.

One warm day when the summer was almost over, Littlenose and Two-Eyes went exploring. They thought there might be some early fruit ripe for eating in the woods farther up the river. They found some brambles and elderberries and ate as many as they could. Then, feeling very sleepy, they lay down in the warm sun in the shelter of a mossy bank. They had been asleep for quite some time when Littlenose woke suddenly to find Two-Eyes standing up, his ears spread wide, and his trunk held out sniffing the breeze.

"What is it, Two-Eyes?" asked Littlenose, but the little mammoth just stood, watching and sniffing. Then, Littlenose's heart almost stopped beating with fright as he saw a movement among some low bushes, and a huge, striped hyena moved slowly out into the sunlight.

Had it seen them? Littlenose decided not to wait to find out. Tugging at Two-Eyes' fur, he started to scramble up the bank . . . and in a moment he'd slid right to the bottom again! Again he tried. And again he slid down. It was so wet and slippery with green moss that he just couldn't keep a grip, while Two-Eyes couldn't even get started.

Littlenose looked around in panic, but there was no other way out. The undergrowth and bushes were thick and thorny, and the only open space was straight ahead, where the hyena now lay with its head in its paws, flicking its ears to drive away the flies, and watching and waiting. Littlenose knew

14

that hyenas were cowardly animals which attacked by creeping up and taking their victims by surprise. He knew that as long as he stayed awake, or as long as it was light, he was safe; but it was already late afternoon and the sun was moving steadily down the sky.

He wondered if they could tip-toe past. But, as soon as they moved away from the bank, the hyena slowly stood up, keeping its eyes firmly fixed on them.

Perhaps he could drive it away. Picking up a stone, Littlenose threw it as hard as he could. But his small arm was not strong enough, the stone fell in the grass, and the hyena hardly glanced at it.

"We'll have to get help, Two-Eyes," said Littlenose. "Now, both together, as loud as you can. One. Two. Three. H-E-L-P!" And Two-Eyes trumpeted and Littlenose shouted as hard as they could.

The hyena jumped back at the sound, and the birds flew out of the trees, screeching with fright. In fact, the birds made so much noise that they quite drowned Littlenose's cries. He shouted himself hoarse, but he soon realised that no one was likely to hear him, certainly neither Mother nor Father back at the cave. If only his voice were strong enough to carry! If only Uncle Redhead were here! He would know what to do.

Uncle Redhead! Of course! Littlenose hardly dared hope. He remembered the day the people had heard the sound of his pipes coming from a distance. He was sure he was no farther away today. He put his hand inside his furs, into the secret pocket where he kept his special treasures, and pulled out his pipes. He had forgotten all about them, and now the hemlock stems had dried and withered to a bruised and bent bundle of dead twigs. Even before he tried, Littlenose knew it was hopeless, but, nevertheless, he put them to his lips and blew . . . and nothing happened.

Littlenose threw down the useless pipes, and looked at the sun, which was level with the tree-tops now. The hyena had also noticed this, and was pacing to and fro. Littlenose watched it, and as he did so his eye caught something white waving gently in the wind. He looked closely. Yes, it was a small clump of hemlock, almost hidden by the long grass and overhanging bushes. And, it was terribly close to the hyena.

Slowly, Littlenose inched his way forward, while the hyena backed away a step or two, waiting to see what would happen. Reaching the clump, Littlenose broke off the thickest stem he could see, and edged his way back to Two-Eyes, never taking his eyes off the hyena.

He had no knife, but he found a sharp stone and began to cut at the hemlock stem as best he could, trying to remember how Uncle Redhead had done it. The result was pretty ragged, but taking an enormous breath, Littlenose put it to his lips and blew with all his might.

At home, Mother was preparing supper, and Father was putting wood on the fire, when suddenly the air was split by a deep booming sound.

"What was that?" said Father, jumping up and dropping sticks all over the place.

The sound came again.

And again!

"It's Littlenose," exclaimed Mother,

"with that thing that Redhead gave him. I thought he'd forgotten all about it."

"I'll give him 'Redhead'," shouted Father. "Why, we'll have the neighbours complaining any minute, and they've only just started speaking to us again." And, leaving the fire, he strode off in the direction of the sound.

It was getting dark when Father at last caught sight of Littlenose who was still frantically blowing. Father was about to rush forward and cuff his ear when he saw a suspicious movement in the long grass. The hyena, feeling bold now in the growing darkness, was creeping up, his mind filled with thoughts of a fine two-course supper of boy and mammoth.

Now, maybe Father didn't know much about music, but he was an expert at throwing stones. Within seconds the hyena's hungry hopes were dashed by a large rock which bounced off his bony skull. Then stones started to rain down on him as if the very sky were falling. Bruised, winded, and yelping with terror, the hyena fled into the night.

As the hyena's howls died in the distance, Littlenose threw himself into his father's arms.

They were about to go when Father bent down and picked up the hemlock stem. "You mustn't forget your pipe," he said. And Littlenose clutched it tightly in his hand as they made their way safely home to Mother.

The Ice Monster

When Littlenose was alive the hills and
woods and rivers looked very much as they
do today. But the great Ice Cap still covered
the northern lands to an enormous depth,
and sent freezing winds sweeping down
throughout the dark winter days. Then,
the Neanderthal folk crouched in their caves
round blazing fires, and passed the time by
telling each other stories. And some of the
best of these stories were about the Ice Cap
itself.

"It is a terrible place," the storyteller
would say. "Long before you even see it the
air gets colder and colder until it hurts to
breathe. The trees get smaller and smaller
until they are no higher than your hand."

"And the Ice Cap?" his listeners would ask.

"It is grim and fearful," the storyteller would continue, "but also strangely beautiful. At daybreak it is a jagged mass of green and blue shadow; at sunset it blazes with crimson fire; and in the noon sun it is so dazzlingly white that a man might go blind from looking at it for more than a short moment. Here is the home of the ice monsters. Few who have seen them have lived to tell of it. It is said that they are taller than ten men, with enormous jaws and long scaly tails, and their roaring can be heard for great distances. Their strength is so great that they hurl boulders of ice down on the heads of anyone foolish enough to venture into their lands."

The storyteller would shudder at the horror of the scene he had just described. And his audience would shudder too, enjoying every word.

Littlenose asked Father about the monsters. "Stuff and nonsense," he snorted.

Then Littlenose asked Uncle Redhead,
who was the cleverest person in the whole
world. "Monsters? Of course there are. I've
seen them."

"Aren't they dangerous?" asked
Littlenose.

"Not them," laughed Uncle Redhead.
"They're too old to harm a mouse. There are
much more dangerous things to beware of at

the Ice Cap than those poor beasts."

Littlenose was very puzzled by his uncle's words. He decided that first thing next morning he would set off for the Ice Cap and see for himself. However, next morning Mother dragged him unwillingly to Old Skinflint the tailor for a new pair of furs. And the day after that he had to go with Father to collect firewood. And then he forgot all about the Ice Cap.

Now, Littlenose's father was an expert hunter, and he was determined that Littlenose would be one too when he grew up. He had promised that Littlenose could accompany a hunting party some day as part of his education, and now that day had arrived.

Littlenose was overjoyed, but Mother wasn't so happy. However, when Father told her it was a horse hunt, she felt better about it. Horses were hunted not for food, but for their skins, which were very valuable.

Hunting horses meant plodding patiently along behind a herd and waiting for a horse to break a leg, or die, or just get left behind, when there was a chance it might become an easy prey. It was far from exciting, but it was fairly safe.

Littlenose set off with his father and the other men early in the morning. They soon found a herd of horses, grazing and wandering slowly in a northerly direction. Keeping carefully down-wind, the hunters followed them . . . for more than a week. A few animals were caught, but not enough, and the hunt went on day after weary day.

Then they lost the horses.

During the night the horses doubled back and by morning were miles away. The men were furious. They all blamed each other, and ran hither and thither, but the horses were out of sight.

"Now," thought Littlenose, "we'll turn back for home."

But among the hunters was a man by the name of Nosey. He was called Nosey because even for a Neanderthal man his nose was exceptionally handsome. And useful. Now he knelt down and sniffed and snuffled among the stones and grass. After a moment he stood up and pointed north. "That's the way they went," he said.

"Are you sure?" asked the others.

"Quite sure," replied Nosey, so they trudged on.

The weather grew colder and the country more bare as the trail took them farther north. They left the trees behind, and were soon travelling over stony ground that was permanently frozen, while an icy wind never stopped blowing. After several days, it was obvious that they had lost all trace of the horses, and that for once Nosey had been wrong. They decided that next morning they would turn back.

But, morning brought a very unpleasant surprise. There was a thick white mist, and the hunters could barely see. Keeping close to each other, they set off in what they hoped was the right direction.

It was late in the afternoon when Father held up his hand and said, "Listen." No one could hear a thing, and they started off again.

"Listen, I can hear something," said Littlenose. And this time they drew together fearfully as out of the mist came a distant low growling. It faded away, then became louder and louder till it was a roar that seemed to fill the air.

"What is it?" said one man. "If only we could see."

"I don't know," said another. "But at least if we can't see it, it can't see us . . . whatever it is."

"I suggest we stay put," said Father. "It'll soon be dark, and we might as well make camp now."

As they did so, it began to get lighter. The mist was clearing, and they were struck dumb by the sight of what lay in front of them. The sun was setting, and the sky was red. They found that they had been marching over a flat, bare plain; but a mile or two in front the plain ended abruptly. Flaming and sparkling like fire against the darkening sky was a great mountain-like mass. It reached half-way to the clouds and stretched far out of sight on either hand. As the sun dropped below the horizon, the colour faded to deep blue and green, and finally to a misty grey as darkness came down.

The hunters watched silently, and again drew closer to one another as the terrible growling and roaring filled the air.

They looked at each other. "The Ice Cap," they said.

"The monsters," said Littlenose.

Nobody slept that night. Apart from the cold, the awful sounds filled the darkness.

When daylight came, things looked a little better. The noises from the Ice Cap stopped, and in the sun its peaks and pinnacles sparkled like a thousand diamonds.

Now that they knew where they were, the hunters could head for home, but first they would have to find some more food, as their supplies were almost used up. Near the camp one of them found the tracks of a herd of musk oxen, so leaving Littlenose in charge, the men set off on the trail.

Littlenose felt quite grown-up. But he soon grew bored. He looked towards the Ice Cap, the main part of which was some way

off. However, the nearest of the broken ice
hummocks was really quite close. There had
been no sound from the ice for a long time.
The monsters must be asleep. Surely going a
little closer could do no harm!

Warily, he walked towards the ice. He
passed the first pieces and went on, stopping
to listen now and again and keeping a careful
watch. But the only sounds were the wind
and the steady drip of water. There was not a
single sign of a monster. Just as he approached
the foot of the Ice Cap proper, he felt a sudden
chill. The sun had disappeared behind a
black cloud. Drops of rain pattered on the ice
and quickly became a downpour.
Littlenose looked about him for shelter, then

started running towards a wide opening in the face of the ice. As he reached it, there came a blinding flash of lightning followed by a peal of thunder which echoed and crashed as if it were the end of the world.

In between flashes, Littlenose's shelter was as black as night; but the lightning glared down through the ice so that the cavern glowed like green and blue fire. A sudden gust of wind blew the rain through the entrance, so Littlenose hurried farther in. When the next flash came he froze with horror.

Towering over him in the flickering light was the most terrible thing he had ever seen. Taller than ten men, with enormous jaws and a long scaly tail, a fearsome animal was poised ready to spring. Littlenose tried to run, but his feet wouldn't move. He just stared, wide-eyed. Then it was dark again, and the horror disappeared. He turned to flee . . . then stopped. His only way of escape was back out of the cave, and the monster would be upon him before he had taken two steps. Perhaps if he stayed absolutely still it would go away.

He crouched down and didn't make a sound. And neither did the monster! Littlenose could hear the drip of water and the sounds of the storm outside the cave, but there was not even the sound of breathing. The monster must have gone.

But if it had, he would surely have heard it move. A huge animal like that was bound to make *some* sound.

Next moment there came the brightest lightning flash of all.

And not only was the monster still there, but its eyes seemed to dart fire at this small creature who had invaded its lair. Littlenose was frantic. He dared not run, but he dared not stay.

The thunder began to die away in the distance as the storm passed, and daylight began to filter into the cave as the dark clouds rolled away.

"It's bound to see me now," thought Littlenose.

But, as the light grew stronger, and he
strained his eyes to peer into the shadows, he
could see nothing! There was no monster.
Just a blank wall of ice. Where had it gone?
He hadn't been dreaming. He *had* seen it,
as tall as ten men, crouched ready to spring;
and there wasn't a crack a mouse could have
hidden in, let alone something *that* big.

At that moment the sun came fully out, and
Littlenose's heart leaped as the awful
creature was suddenly there again . . . but it
didn't move, and Littlenose saw why. It was
frozen into the ice. Like the small fish he had
sometimes seen in the river in winter, the
creature was imprisoned and harmless. How
many thousands of years it had remained
like that he had no way of knowing, but now
he understood Uncle Redhead's words about
the ice monsters being too old to harm
anyone. Hunters who had been frightened
as he had been had made up the tales told
round the fires. The roaring and growling

must simply be pieces of ice breaking and falling from the Ice Cap . . . not being thrown down by anyone or anything.

What a story this was going to make when he got back!

"Goodbye, poor old monster," he said softly, and left the cavern.

He didn't tell his father or any of the hunting party. He decided to save it till he got home. But when he did try to tell of his adventure, no one would listen. In fact, he was scolded by Father for having left the camp unguarded.

Only Uncle Redhead believed him, and he, after all, was the cleverest person in the whole world.

Littlenose and the Beavers

Almost the most important job in the days
when Littlenose lived was the gathering of
firewood. Every family kept a fire burning
near the front of its cave. The caves had no
doors, and hungry bears and tigers were
afraid of flames and the smell of a fire. It was
a great calamity when the fire went out, and
so firewood was always kept handy.

Littlenose's home was a snug cave among
some tumbled rocks close by a broad,
slow-flowing river. The few trees which had
grown nearby when the family moved in had
been burnt long ago. One evening, Father
threw a log on the fire and said, "Well, that's
almost the last. Tomorrow, we must go and
look for more wood."

"Me too?" asked Littlenose.

"You too," replied Father, without much enthusiasm. Littlenose had a knack of turning a simple task into a disaster!

"Two-Eyes had better come," went on Father. "He has a strong back, and he can carry much more than we can."

Early next morning, the wood-gatherers set off. Father led the way along the river bank, making for a spot where a small stream flowed out of a narrow glen. There was usually lots of driftwood to be found here, and Father reasoned that if they followed the stream they would find out where the wood came from. Then they could collect firewood when it was needed, instead of waiting for the stream to wash it down.

It was warm on the open river bank and clouds of midges flew around their heads. Littlenose wished that he had a beard like Father's. The midges could hardly *see* his face, let alone bite it. However, when they turned

away to follow the small stream, they left
the midges behind. They also left the sun.
The glen was narrow and thickly-wooded,
and the air was cool and dim.

They quickly lost sight of the river, and
only occasionally caught a glimpse of the sky
through the branches.

They walked and walked. They passed
masses of wood lying in piles along both
banks, as well as caught in low overhanging
tree branches. Littlenose was certain that he
could have loaded Two-Eyes several times
over by now and gone home, but, when he
mentioned this, Father only grunted and
pressed on.

The glen began to open out. The stream
became broader and there were some pools.
Father peered into one pool where trout were
darting, grunted: "Lunch," and carried on.
However, after a few moments Littlenose's
miserable expression became too much for
him, and he said, "We'll stop now. It's about

noon. I'll catch some fish, and you collect
wood for a fire.''

Littlenose cheered up at once. He looked
around him for a moment . . . and stopped in
astonishment. There was no wood! Not a
single twig! He thought of all the lovely wood
he had passed earlier. There weren't even any
trees growing nearby. He would have to go
and search.

"Come on, Two-Eyes," Littlenose called.
''If there's no firewood, there'll be no lunch,''
and together they scampered up the bank.

Almost immediately they saw trees.

Some distance upstream, they could see a
birch wood. There would be plenty of fallen
branches *there*. Keeping his eye on the tree
tops, Littlenose led Two-Eyes upstream.

39

The birch wood was further off than Littlenose had imagined, and by the time he reached the first trees, he was very hot. He sat down to rest.

Peering through the trees, he could see sunlight. "There must be a clearing," he thought. He could see the now tiny stream shining among the shadows, and it seemed to flow through the clearing. But something was not quite right! Littlenose got up and walked carefully forward. There was a sort of high bank right across the clearing, and the stream seemed to spring from the foot of it. There was something odd about the bank, too. It was not earth. And it was not rock. It was made of *tree-trunks!* Yes, tree-trunks. Dozens and dozens of the slender trunks of birch trees were interwoven and interlaced with twigs and smaller branches. The stream emerged from under the bank as hundreds of little rivulets. But, what was even stranger, these branches had not got here by accident.

They were not broken . . . but *cut!* Cut neatly, as though by many blows of a flint axe. The bank had been built by someone. The Straightnoses, perhaps? Some of the cut wood was very fresh indeed. Perhaps the builders were still nearby.

Littlenose began to feel afraid. He had forgotten all about the firewood. He really ought to hurry back and find Father . . . but he must have just *one* look at what lay beyond the bank. It was easy to scramble up the tangled trunks and branches, and in a moment he stood on top.

He was not sure what he had expected to find, and his eyes popped wide with astonishment. On one side, Two-Eyes waited patiently in the clearing. On the other side, a wide expanse of calm water stretched between the trees, and lapped the bank at his feet. In the tall grass at the water's edge, he could see the stumps of birch trees which had been cut down, and piles of fresh wood chips showed white in the sun.

But there were no signs of people.

Littlenose was about to turn away, when a movement caught his eye. One of the birch trees was waving gently . . . yet there was no wind! As he watched, it leaned farther and farther over, until, with a thump and a shower of leaves it fell to the ground.

Littlenose was petrified. He stared
wide-eyed at the spot where the top of the
fallen tree could just be seen over the tall
grass . . . and it began to move!

Slowly, jerkily, with much crunching of
leaves and crackling of twigs, the tree was
travelling towards the water. Several times it
stopped as if to rest, but eventually it slid out
of the grass, down a wet, muddy slope and
into the water.

And Littlenose suddenly felt very relieved
and thrilled at the same time. Uncle Redhead
had once described an animal he had seen on

his travels. It was large and furry, with a broad tail and big teeth. Father had snorted with disbelief as Uncle Redhead had told how these animals lived in burrows with under-water entrances. They even cut down trees, he said, and built dams across streams to form deep water lakes around their homes. Uncle Redhead called them beavers.

And here they were! An animal just like Uncle Redhead's description was tugging and pushing the fallen tree into deeper water. It had been hidden by the long grass while it was felling the tree. Another beaver swam to join the first, and together they towed the trunk towards the dam. There they proceeded to poke and push it into place. They ignored Littlenose, who watched as they snipped here, nibbled there, and gradually wove the new material into the old. They cut the wood easily with their large teeth. What useful things, thought Littlenose. Much better than a flint axe for cutting firewood, for instance.

Firewood!

Oh, dear! He'd done it again. He'd forgotten what he was supposed to be fetching.

Shouting to Two-Eyes, he dashed along the top of the dam towards the trees, startling the beavers, who disappeared under the water.

"Quick, Two-Eyes," he panted, "we've got to pick up sticks," and he started gathering an armful of dry branches and wood chips.

Two-Eyes didn't feel like dashing about. After all, there was plenty of wood where he was. He chose a nice big piece and wrapped his trunk around it. It was rather awkward, so he took a firmer grip, braced his short little legs, and pulled.

At that moment, Littlenose came out of the trees. He took one horrified look.

"Oh, no, Two-Eyes," he shouted. "Not that one! Put it down!"

But Two-Eyes didn't hear. He had made up his mind to have this branch, and nothing was going to stop him. What he hadn't noticed

was that this stick was an important part of
the beavers' dam, which was beginning to
creak alarmingly as he heaved and strained.

Water started gushing out of the dam in a
dozen places, and loose branches were
beginning to break away.

"Stop, Two-Eyes," cried Littlenose,
"before it's too late!"

Two-Eyes paused for breath. A spray of
water splashed over his fur, and he jumped –
not a moment too soon.

With a snapping and cracking of tree
branches, a whole section of the dam slowly
collapsed and, in a rushing brown torrent,

the waters of the little lake poured across the clearing, through the birch wood, and down the bed of the stream.

While Littlenose had been watching the beavers, Father had caught several fine trout for lunch, and was now waiting for the wood for a fire to cook them. When Littlenose did not appear, Father, muttering to himself about young people and their lack of responsibility, started poking about and eventually collected a few pieces of rather damp drift-wood and twigs. He took out his flints, and started striking sparks. But because the wood was damp, it took a great deal of effort to produce even a pale flicker of flame and a thin thread of smoke. Father sat back. His hands were sore from striking flints, and his cheeks ached from blowing. It was a very small fire, but it would do until Littlenose brought more fuel. Father stood up to look for him.

He had a quick glimpse of a muddy wave of water rushing down on him before he was bowled head over heels.

Littlenose and Two-Eyes hurried back to where they had left Father. "We've got to warn him," Littlenose panted as he ran.

They reached what they thought was the place, but it looked different. Where was he? The grass was wet and flattened, and the stream had become swift and muddy. Littlenose ran along the bank, calling: "Father! Father, where are you?"

He reached the edge of the woods before he heard Father's voice from the branches of a tree!

"Just wait until I get down," he shouted angrily. "You've been up to your tricks again. This is all your fault." And he jumped to the ground in a great tangle of broken branches and other rubbish swept along by the flood.

Poor Littlenose! Father just wouldn't let him explain that it wasn't really his fault. He wouldn't even listen to his wonderful story of the beavers. He just loaded up Two-Eyes with some very soggy firewood, and set off gloomily for home.

And the beavers?

They set out immediately to cut down some more birch trees, and soon their dam and their pond were as good as new.

Littlenose's Voyage

Littlenose loved the river. It flowed past the cave where he lived with Father and Mother and Two-Eyes. The river flowed smoothly, except when the snow melted in the spring; then its surface was broken by curling waves which reminded Littlenose of the sea. Then, too, the river brought down trees, bushes and even dead animals, and carried them swiftly past and far away.

One hot summer day, Littlenose was stretched out in the long grass watching the river. The sun was shining, insects hummed, and Two-Eyes lazily flapped his ears from time to time to drive them away.

The place where Littlenose lay was a long sand-spit which reached out from the bank, ending in a small patch of beach. Littlenose lay above the beach and imagined himself floating along on the river.

He watched a fallen tree caught in a tangle of dead branches, which bobbed gently in the current.

"I wonder where that came from?" he thought. "And will it end up as firewood in somebody's cave? Or will it float all the way to the sea, and be lost for ever?" He turned to Two-Eyes. But Two-Eyes had gone.

Littlenose decided that he too might as well go home. It seemed a long time since lunch, and he might manage a small snack if Mother were about . . . or a large one if she weren't. He walked along to where the dark woods came down to the river's edge.

And there he met the bear!

Luckily, he saw it first.

Under the trees were patches of black shadow and, as Littlenose approached, one of the patches suddenly rose up, stretched,

and gave an enormous yawn. It was a huge
black bear. It had been sleeping in the cool
of the woods when Littlenose's footsteps had
disturbed it. Now it stood, still half-asleep,
peering blearily and wondering what was
happening. Littlenose didn't wait for it to
find out. He ran away as fast as he could.

After a moment he looked back. The bear
was turning its head this way and that and for
a moment Littlenose thought it was going
to sleep. But instead it dropped on all fours
and came swiftly towards him.

Littlenose ran even faster this time. Out

along the sand-spit he fled, with the bear in
hot pursuit. Across the beach he went. The
river was on three sides of him, with the bear
rushing up on the fourth.

He was trapped. No, not quite.

Quickly he splashed into the shallow water,
scrambled through the tangled branches
of the fallen tree, and climbed on to
the trunk. The tree rocked alarmingly as the
bear tried to follow Littlenose, but the
branches were too close together for it to
get at him.

Again and again the bear tried to pull
itself up, but the dead branches broke under
its weight. Littlenose clung on as far as
possible from the furious animal.

Then the bear made one more effort. It
drew back and stood snarling, water
streaming from its fur and eyes ablaze with
rage, then it threw itself forward with a roar.
It lunged madly at the log and seized a
branch with both paws. It had pulled itself

partly on to the log before the branch gave way, and it fell back with a loud splash. The tree rocked and rolled wildly, but Littlenose hung on grimly and saw the bear swimming back to the shore.

He was safe. Or, was he?

The bear was *swimming!*

The tree was no longer aground in shallow water, but had drifted out from the shore. Already the current was beginning to carry it downstream, and Littlenose watched the beach get farther and farther away. He could hardly make out the sand-spit now, and couldn't see the bear at all. The last thing he saw before the current carried him round a bend was a trickle of smoke from the cave.

"Oh, dear," he thought, "I'm going to be late for supper." But he wasn't very worried. He was sure that the log would soon drift towards the shore.

However, as the afternoon passed, the log kept a steady course down the middle of the river. He no longer had any idea where he was. Thick woods lined either bank, and he could see no sign of life. He began to think of all the rubbish he often watched floating past the cave. He had wondered where it went. Now, he was going to find out.

Littlenose looked left and right, and tried to judge whether the log was drifting towards one shore or the other. Then he noticed he was coming to a line of trees and bushes. "The river must bend," he thought. "I'll soon be ashore!" The log drifted on slowly now, but the gap narrowed all the time.

At last Littlenose was almost within touching distance of the trees. The log sailed gently along the shore. Then an eddy swung the log around and its roots caught in the low-hanging branches of a willow. It stopped, rocking gently. Carefully, Littlenose inched his way along the trunk, and pulled himself into the tree. In a moment he was on dry land at last!

Littlenose looked about him. Then he pushed his way through the thick bushes to a narrow sandy path. It was patterned with the tracks of animals, but as it seemed to be nothing larger than rabbits, he decided it was safe. So he set off along the path in what he hoped was the direction of home.

But it didn't appear to be the direction of anywhere. He could just see patches of sky above him, and the undergrowth on either side seemed endless. The air was hot, and the sand dragged at his feet. Littlenose felt he must sit down for a little while, so he settled down against a tree and looked up at the sky.

Suddenly, he sat up with a jerk and blinked. What had happened? The air was cooler. The shadows were darker. And the sky above his head was no longer blue . . . but pink! He must have fallen asleep. He would have to hurry to be home before dark.

He started to run, but stumbled in the soft, churned sand. As the light faded, Littlenose

had to watch carefully where he was going.
He ran with head bent, peering anxiously at
the ground. And then he had another
unpleasant surprise. Something other than
rabbits had made prints in *this* sand. There
were tracks of a larger creature – deep tracks,
and the sand was scattered as if the animal
were in a great hurry. Littlenose stopped and
listened. There were soft chirps and scuffles
from the bushes, but nothing that sounded
like a large animal. But at least the creature
was in front – he was safe if he didn't catch up
with it. He started walking again, watching
carefully, hoping the strange trail might turn
off into the trees.

But it didn't. Instead, Littlenose saw that the first creature seemed to have been joined by a second. There was a double line of deep, scuffling prints in the sand. Littlenose didn't know what to do. He had no idea what sort of creature he was following – there might even be a whole herd of them! Then a thought struck him. He bent down and looked closely at the ground. The larger footprints looked like his own.

And then the horrible truth dawned. They *were* his own! He had been walking in circles.

And, if he had been walking in circles with the river always on one side of him, it could mean only one thing. He had not landed on the river bank. He had landed on an island! He must get off – but how? There was only one way. The log – if it were still there. Without wasting another moment, Littlenose pushed through to the water. The floating trunk was still caught by its roots, and Littlenose lay along a branch and broke

away most of the tangled twigs before dropping down on to the log. His weight did the rest. With a frightening roll and lurch, the log drifted out into the current.

On and on he drifted. The air was beginning to chill as the sun moved steadily down the western sky. It grew even colder as the log swung around a bend.

Littlenose shivered, and as he did so he noticed that the river banks were closing in, and the current was beginning to run more swiftly. And the water was choppy, with small waves which made the tree-trunk roll.

Littlenose clung on hard. The waves became bigger, and he was buffeted and spun one way and the other.

It was getting darker every moment, too, and Littlenose thought: "If only I drift into the bank while I can still see, I might just jump ashore safely," and at that moment the log gave a particularly violent lurch and swung towards the shore. Littlenose watched anxiously as the bank came nearer, but, to his dismay he drifted to within a few yards and then moved away again. But it didn't make much difference. The bank was a smooth, rocky cliff, impossible to climb.

Back into the main stream raced the log. Littlenose hung on, lying astride the rough trunk, his eyes tight shut as the waves poured over him and he expected to be swept off any moment.

Littlenose looked up as the tree jarred on a rock. Some yards away was the bank, but again it was a smooth rock face.

60

He looked again. It was the same rock face!

He had been round in a complete circle!
Already he was being carried out again, and
he was moving much faster. In a few moments
he was back where he had started, but farther
from the shore. Again and again the current
carried the log in a circle, but the circle was a
little smaller each time. What was
happening? Where was the river taking him?

He raised himself to get a better view, and
in the last of the light a dreadful sight met his
eyes. Now, he *knew* what happened to
anything carried down by the river. He was
being swept towards the centre of an
enormous whirlpool. The water roared as it
raced in foaming circles around a dark pit in
the centre. As Littlenose watched, a large

leafy branch was swept into the middle and vanished, sucked beneath the black water.

Littlenose shuddered.

That's what would happen to him if he didn't do something quickly. But what could he do? Jumping off the log wouldn't help. He had to get to the bank. He was moving so fast that he was dizzy, and he could look right down into the dark mouth of the whirlpool. He watched another branch disappear, and as he did so he almost fell into the water as something cold brushed against his shoulder.

He looked, but couldn't see anything.

Could it be a monster living in the whirlpool? Then it happened again! This time he was able to glimpse something against the night sky. It was the branch of a tree, reaching out over the river, and it *might* just bear his weight.

The log was approaching the branch again, and Littlenose sprang up as he passed under it. But then the log rolled under him. He

managed to grab a handful of twigs, and the
next moment he was in the water. He only
just managed to scramble out as the branch
passed over-head again, and he was too late
to catch it. But now he stood up carefully, and
balanced himself on the rocking log, which
was already on the smooth slope of water
leading to the centre of the whirlpool. He
kept his eyes on the dark, shadowy shape of
the branch against the sky, and as it rushed
past he reached up with both hands and took
a firm grip.

Instantly, he was up to his waist in water as
the log shot from under him, and the branch
bent under his weight. Desperately, he
dragged himself up hand over hand while the

current tore at his legs and almost pulled his arms from his shoulders. At length he reached a fork in the branch and was able to rest for a moment. Below him, in the faint starlight, he caught a last glimpse of his log as it spun furiously on end, like a huge club brandished by a giant hand, before disappearing into the centre of the whirlpool.

Littlenose shivered. He had almost gone the same way. And he wasn't safe yet. He still had to reach solid ground, and he didn't know where he was.

The climb down to the ground was fairly easy, and soon Littlenose was on top of the cliff, with the river roaring far below. He gathered some dry sticks, and took his flints from the secret pocket inside his furs. Rubbing the flints dry, he managed to strike a spark and get a fire started. Then he curled up in a hollow to sleep.

The sound of voices awoke Littlenose, and he opened his eyes. Mother, Father and

Two-Eyes were standing beside him. He was home! Had it all been a dream?

No, the scratches on his arms and the wet furs drying over the fire were quite real.

"How did I get here?" he asked.

"Have your breakfast, and I'll show you," said Father, and as soon as Littlenose had eaten, Father took him on to the high hill which lay behind the cave. After a short walk he pointed, and Littlenose saw the charred twigs of his fire. A few more paces, and they were gazing down at the whirlpool far below. It looked even more frightening in daylight.

And Littlenose saw for the first time that the river flowed in a wide loop around his home. His adventurous voyage had ended only a short distance from the cave, on the other side of the hill, where Father had found him. He felt rather silly about it all, but even so, it was a long time before he next went to play by the river.

Littlenose the Hero

It was a wet afternoon, and Littlenose was bored. He was also in disgrace. Father wagged a finger at him and exclaimed: "That's the last time you come hunting with me. To think of it. In front of all those men. I'm surprised that they still speak to me. You ought to hang your head in shame."

But Littlenose didn't. He wasn't even listening particularly. He was used to this sort of thing. "We'll get the 'when I was your age' bit any minute," he thought.

"When I was your age," went on Father, "I was the sole support of my old mother. I was an expert hunter, and my spear-throwing was the talk of the whole tribe."

Actually, Littlenose's was too; but only

because when Father had tried to teach him he had succeeded in hurling a spear through a neighbour's best furs which had been hung out to dry.

All this lecturing by Father had come about because he really *was* a first-class hunter. What's more, he wanted Littlenose to be one too when he grew up. Now, there were no schools in those days, and a boy had to rely on his parents for everything he needed to learn. Sometimes this was very boring, but sometimes it could be more exciting than any school. Father had already taken Littlenose on hunting trips, but this last one had been different. Littlenose had been allowed to help instead of just looking on.

Father continued with his lecture. "There must be something you can get right," he said despairingly. "When we let you do the tracking you led us right into a lions' den; and we only got away because the camp fire we asked you to light set the forest ablaze and we managed to escape in the smoke. I just don't know!" And he gazed sadly into the fire.

Poor Littlenose! He really did try hard. He really did want to grow up to be as good a hunter as Father. Of course, that was part of the trouble. Father was just too good. Why couldn't *he* make the occasional mistake? People weren't usually right *all* the time. Except Father, that is. He had a wonderful day-dream in which Father was surrounded by wild animals, including at least three woolly rhinoceros, and only he, Littlenose, could save him; which he did with great dash and bravery and so became the hero of the

tribe. But he knew that it would more likely end with his being chased up a tree or eaten by something.

Littlenose went to bed that night very downcast, and over breakfast next morning he sat silently and thought and thought. There must be some way he could show Father that he wasn't as stupid as everyone imagined. He was still thinking as he went out to play with Two-Eyes, and didn't even notice one man call jokingly to his wife, "Watch the washing! Here comes the spear champion!" or another who was trying to light a fire and cried, "Come and help, Littlenose! You can light bigger fires than any of us!"

Littlenose spent most of the morning sitting under his favourite tree with Two-Eyes, and eventually thought of a plan. He decided that Father was not going to get into a tight fix and require rescuing just to suit him. If he were to prove himself as a great

hunter, then he must hunt something . . . all
by himself. Then he would show them!
What to hunt, and how, was the problem.
The Neanderthal folk had several methods,
and Littlenose considered all of them.
Firstly, small game, birds and rabbits were
killed with sticks and stones. But Littlenose's
stick and stone throwing was at the best of
times unreliable. Secondly, horses and deer
were either stalked and speared, or chased
and stampeded over a high rock. But, once
again, Littlenose's stalking was most likely to
cause a stampede, and as for chasing, the
animals usually got the wrong idea altogether
and chased Littlenose instead!

"However," he thought, "if I'm going to

be a great hunter, I want to hunt something really big. Like a rhinoceros."

He had heard his father speak of how some tribes had caught these huge, bad-tempered creatures. First, they dug a large hole in the ground. Then, they covered the hole with tree branches and leaves and grass, until no one would ever suspect that the ground wasn't solid, and neither would the rhinoceros. When one came along, the branches broke under its weight, and it fell into the hole. It was beautifully simple. What happened next, like getting the rhinoceros out of the hole and taking it home, was something that Littlenose didn't even consider.

First thing after lunch he started digging. He had a spade made from a flat bone tied to a stick, and found it much harder work than he had imagined. There were rocks to be moved, and tree roots to be chopped through. His arms and shoulders ached, but by supper-time he had something to show for all his effort. The hole was at least knee-deep. Carefully, he hid his spade in some bushes and went home.

Mother was appalled when she saw him. "What have you been doing?" she exclaimed, as he trotted into the cave.

"Just playing," said Littlenose. "Is supper ready?"

"There's no supper for you, young man, until you scrub all that dirt off, *and* change your furs. You're absolutely filthy. I just don't know how you do it!"

At bedtime it was the same. Littlenose came home even dirtier.

In the days and weeks that followed, Mother became very worried about Littlenose. He was out of bed every morning as soon as it was light, instead of having to be dragged out. Except for meal times, he was out of the cave all day, instead of having to be chased out every few minutes by Mother while she tried to get on with her housework.

Except for his getting so dirty, he was like a new boy!

Meanwhile, the hole was getting bigger. Knee-deep, then waist-deep, then shoulder-deep. Soon, Littlenose couldn't see out as he dug, but he kept on. A rhinoceros was a very big creature and the trap must be large enough. Littlenose was also worried in case someone should find out what he was doing. He wanted it to be a surprise when he arrived home with his rhinoceros.

At last, the hole was finished. Now came the next part of the work. Littlenose searched the woods round about, and collected all the fallen branches he could see. With Two-Eyes' help, he laid them across the hole in all directions until it was completely covered. Then he spread dead leaves and grass over the branches, and sprinkled earth over that, until you would never have guessed that a deep pit lay underneath.

All he needed now was a rhinoceros.

Looking at the sun, Littlenose realised that it was getting late. It was long past supper-time. He had better hurry. He gave a last artistic sprinkling of grass to his rhinoceros trap, and ran with Two-Eyes in the direction of home.

Mother was furious when he reached the cave.

"Littlenose," she shrieked, "you get more exasperating every day. Where have you been? Father's gone to look for you. You'd better run after him and call him back, or he'll be out all night."

Littlenose ran out of the cave to look for Father. He went along by the river, up on the hill, and into the woods. But there was no sign of him. He decided that Father must already have gone home, and that he had better do likewise or he would be in trouble.

He had only taken a few steps, however, when he heard a dreadful commotion. It sounded like a very large and very angry

animal. He looked quickly for a handy tree
to climb, then stopped. The sounds weren't
getting any nearer. He listened again . . . and
his heart leaped!

His trap! It had worked! He had caught
something!

Littlenose ran as quickly as he could. The
noises coming from the hole when he reached
it were blood-curdling. He dropped on to all
fours and crept carefully forward. The
shadows in the pit made it difficult to see
much, but as his eyes grew accustomed to the
dim light, he saw, covered with earth, dead

leaves and grass, and roaring with rage as he tried to climb out . . . Father!

For a dreadful moment there was silence. Then Father bellowed, "Don't just stand there! Get me out!"

Littlenose looked around. He saw a slender sapling growing by the pit. "Don't go away, Father. I'll be back," he said, and dashed away in the direction of home.

Mother was startled when Littlenose rushed into the cave, seized an axe and rushed out again. Back at the trap, he quickly chopped through the stem of the sapling, so that it toppled over with one end in the hole. In a moment Father had scrambled up and out.

76

Littlenose had just decided to run when,
to his astonishment, there was a great burst
of cheering.

All the men of the tribe were gathered
round, and before he could move, he felt
himself lifted up on to broad shoulders and
carried at the head of a torchlight procession.
The men sang as they marched, and at last
Littlenose found himself set down in front of
the Old Man, the leader of the tribe. He put
his hand on Littlenose's head and made a
long speech, most of which Littlenose didn't
understand. He just stood in a daze in front
of everyone. He could see Father with a very
odd expression on his face, and Mother
smiling with tears streaming down her cheeks

as the Old Man concluded his speech with,
" . . . and so, to a brave lad who, as befits the
son of a great hunter, saved his father from
the perils of the dark forest, I present this
token." And he handed Littlenose a boy-sized
hunting spear.

Once again, everybody cheered, this time
shouting: "Speech! Speech!"

But Littlenose only smiled happily and said, "Thank you."

And so Littlenose became a hero, not that it made any real difference. He was still Littlenose, the naughty boy of the tribe, and even if he *had* rescued Father from the rhinoceros trap, Father had a pretty good idea whose fault it was that he had required rescuing in the first place. Also, people soon stopped saying things like *A Hero Wouldn't Do This*, or *A Hero Wouldn't Do That*. Even the spear presented by the Old Man lay forgotten at the back of the cave. In almost no time at all Littlenose and Two-Eyes were playing happily together with no thoughts of brave deeds, but simply having fun. And that is much more important for small boys and mammoths.